WEAKLY WORMIT
AND THE
ESCAPE OF THE GOBBLERS

Fiona Hunter

Illustrations by James Byrne

Grosvenor House
Publishing Limited

This book is published by
Grosvenor House Publishing Ltd
Link House
140 The Broadway, Tolworth, Surrey, KT6 7HT.
www.grosvenorhousepublishing.co.uk

This book is a work of fiction. Any resemblance to
people or events, past or present, is purely coincidental.

A CIP record for this book
is available from the British Library

ISBN 978-1-80381-139-0

Everyone hates bullying.

So did Wormit.

This is how he learnt to be brave and show

the bullies that he was better than they were.

Wormit did not always have green hair. To begin with, he was a very ordinary boy, or so you might have thought, who lived with his parents Mr and Mrs MacDermitt.

Mrs MacDermitt was a very busy lady who scrubbed and cleaned all day and never took much notice of poor Wormit.

Mr MacDermitt spent most of his time writing in his study. He wrote very bad poetry and always talked in rhyme. For example, he might say,

"What will it be? What will it be?
What are we going to have for tea?"

Mrs MacDermitt would never reply because she was so busy with her housework and she did not much like poetry. When their little son was born Mrs MacDermitt wanted to call him John which she said was a fine name. Mr MacDermitt said,

"It may be fine but it doesn't rhyme!
We'll call him Wormit, Wormit MacDermitt."

Mrs MacDermitt was not so sure, and when he brought home a wriggly kitten for the new baby and called it Squirmit MacDermitt she was very cross.

Years went by and it was time for their little son to go to school. Wormit was excited and happy. He did not know that Wormit MacDermitt was a peculiar name. When he got to school the children laughed at him because of his name and they danced around him saying,

"Wormit MacDermitt, Wormit MacDermitt."

That was bad enough but before long they noticed that he was small and skinny. Soon they were calling him Weakly Wormit MacDermitt. Of course this made poor Wormit sad and he longed to be big and strong.

One day, he read a story about a man who was big and strong because he ate spinach. Wormit felt sure that this would work for him and it just so happened that there was a field of spinach nearby.

Wormit decided to eat the spinach raw and he climbed the gate into the field and tasted a leaf of spinach. It was horrid. It would have been nice cooked with a little butter and chopped onion and pepper, but Wormit was convinced that there was no time to lose. He sat for hours eating spinach. He began to feel sick but was determined to be strong and he made himself eat more.

At last he went home and dashed upstairs to look at himself in the long mirror. Would he be bigger? Would he be stronger? Oh no!......Oh horror!.....What a shock he got! He was not really any bigger, but, and it was a terrible "but", his hair had turned green, a deep and brilliant green, the very colour of spinach.

When his father Mr MacDermitt saw him he said,

"Where have you been? Where have you been?
Why is your hair that horrible green?"

His mother rushed him to the bathroom and she scrubbed and scrubbed his hair muttering to herself about more work, but his hair stayed green, very green.

Poor Wormit was especially sad that day and Squirmit went to school with him at least as far as the school gate to help him to be brave because green hair was not an excuse for staying off school. As soon as he got in the gate the children gathered round him and started to chant,

"Weakly Wormit's got green hair, Weakly Wormit's got green hair!"

This went on for a few days but then something happened that was to change Wormit's whole life. A girl with long golden hair took pity on Wormit.

"Hello" she said. "What a lovely cat" and she stroked Squirmit. "What's his name?"

"Squirmit" said Wormit.

"Hello Squirmit" said the girl with the golden hair. "Would you like to come to play in my garden, you and Wormit? I am Isabelinda by the way."

Squirmit looked at Isabelinda with a cat smile and purred.

"We would love to….." said Wormit.

So after school they went to Isabelinda's garden. It was a big garden with grass in the middle and all around it there was a wood. When they were playing hide and seek, Wormit found a strange old stone shed with no windows and only a heavy door with a big rusty handle and a keyhole. There was no key. Wormit tried the door but it was locked.

"It's very old" said Isabelinda when she found him. "It has always been locked. Nobody ever goes in there".

"Why not?" asked Wormit.

"I think there might be something bad inside" said Isabelinda, "but I think I know where they key might be."

Sure enough, on the inside of the backdoor of her house, there was a bunch of keys of all different sizes. They examined the keys. Some of them looked very old.

"Let's try to get in!" said Isabelinda.

"Miaow!" said Squirmit which meant "No – I'm scared."

"I don't think we should" said Wormit "if there is something bad inside."

Sometimes people do silly things when they are curious, and afterwards they are sorry. This was one of those times.

"Come on!" urged Isabelinda.

"Oh alright" replied Wormit but he was worried especially as the fur on Squirmit's back was standing on end and he was hissing at the shed door.

"Don't worry Squirmit" said Wormit nervously as they tried all the keys. At first they thought none of them would fit, but at last they tried a huge rusty key and it turned in the lock.

"Will we?" asked Isabelinda.

"Alright" said Wormit.

"Miaow" squealed Squirmit and shot under a bush.

They turned the handle looking at each other with big eyes.

"CREAK" went the door as it opened……..Out, with a terrible noise of hissing and rasping and flapping of wings and with black fury flew the Gobblers.

Shut inside for a hundred years and unable to eat the one thing they longed for – human hair.

With their open beaks and crocodile teeth and ferocious eyes they dived on Wormit and Isabelinda, and they grabbed with their claws and teeth huge lumps of Isabelinda's beautiful golden hair and tore at it till she was quite bald.

They hissed and dived on Wormit but oddly they left his hair quite untouched. Suddenly they flew squawking into the sky making it black with their beating wings.

They flew round and round looking for more hair. People in the village ran for their houses but most were too late. The Gobblers swooped on everyone and with their long beaks and clawing feet gobbled up people's hair, yellow hair, golden hair, auburn hair, red hair, brown hair, black hair and white hair, straight hair and curly hair.

Nearly everyone in the village was bald and everyone was too frightened to go outside. Mr MacDermitt was caught while strolling in the garden making up rhymes. So great was the shock he shouted out,

"Hey there! Where is my hair?
Where is my hair, oh where?
Bring back my hair, I'm in despair
It's so unfair, too much to bear
Beasts of the air, where is my hair?
Where is my hair? Oh where?"

Isabelinda cried and cried.

"It was all my fault" she said. Tears ran down her cheeks as she put her hands up to her bald head.

"Why didn't they eat your hair?" she asked.

"I don't know" replied Wormit. "They didn't seem to like green hair."

Wormit said goodbye to Isabelinda very kindly and told her that he was going to catch the Gobblers. He found Squirmit shivering under a bush, put him inside his shirt, and went home.

He had no idea how to catch the Gobblers, but he knew that he must help the people in the village all locked up in their homes, too frightened to come out. Nobody went to work, nobody went to school and nobody went shopping. Soon people began to get hungry because they had no food.

Wormit went to the shop a long way away in town to buy food and took it to everyone's houses; he dug cabbages, carrots and potatoes, he collected eggs, and did everything he could to help until he became tired with all the work.

Everyone was grateful and watched out for Wormit's green head passing their windows. Now everyone called him "Wonderful Wormit". The Gobblers circled in the sky above, black and scary, but they left Wormit alone.

At last he thought of a plan. When he was in town getting shopping for the people of the village he bought a yellow wig from the hairdresser's shop. He put it at the bottom of the shopping basket so that it was quite hidden. He explained his plan to Squirmit who came up and rubbed his silky coat against Wormit.

"Miaow" he said, which means "Good luck".

So Wormit set out for Isabelinda's garden with the yellow wig hidden under his shirt. He opened wide the Gobblers' shed door and found himself a long stick. Inside the shed he tied the wig to the stick and then, holding the stick to his chest, with the wig on top of the stick so that it flowed in long yellow curls and hid his own green hair, he strode out bravely to the middle of the lawn.

The Gobblers dived immediately, hungry for the bright yellow hair. Wormit ran towards the shed. The gobblers were tearing at the wig and with all his strength Wormit hurled the stick into the shed. A black cloud of flapping Gobblers clung furiously to the wig. As quick as a flash Wormit slammed the door. He looked around. Every Gobbler had gone.

Wormit locked the door with the big heavy key, when he had done that he found a spade and dug a deep hole and dropped the key to the very bottom. Then he covered up the hole.

Wormit went to tell Isabelinda. Soon everyone in the village knew what had happened and came out onto the street and danced with happiness. Even Mrs MacDermitt stopped working for five minutes. Mr MacDermitt was quiet for a long time because he wanted to write a poem and he couldn't think of anything to rhyme with Gobblers so instead he had to content himself with:

> *"Well done my son, not bad, not bad*
> *You're nearly as clever as your Dad."*

He could not think of anything else that would rhyme except:

> *"What's for tea, what's for tea?*
> *I hope it's something good for me."*

Wormit didn't mind. He could go with Squirmit to play in Isabelinda's garden whenever he wanted. Very soon her hair grew back long and golden, and before long the green faded from his own hair, and nobody, but nobody, laughed at him again.

CPSIA information can be obtained
at www.ICGtesting.com
Printed in the USA
LVHW070825030822
725020LV00019B/569